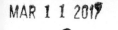

W9-AHF-158

○ PUPPY ACADEMY ○

STAR
on Stormy Mountain

X

Gill Lewis

illustrations by Sarah Horne

Henry Holt and Company ✽ New York

Welcome to Sausage Dreams Puppy Academy, where a team of plucky young pups are learning how to be all sorts of working dogs. Let's meet some of the students . . .

STAR
the speedy one!

BREED: Border collie

SPECIAL SKILL:
Sensing danger

Crazy ~~about~~ puppies!

Ready for big adventure?

Want to know about real-life working dogs?

"Gill Lewis, a former vet, is a major talent."

—THE TIMES (UK)

No sheep were harmed in the making of this book.

Henry Holt and Company, LLC, *Publishers since 1866*
175 Fifth Avenue, New York, New York 10010
mackids.com

Library of Congress Cataloging-in-Publication Data
Names: Lewis, Gill, author. | Horne, Sarah, illustrator.
Title: Star on Stormy Mountain / Gill Lewis ; illustrations by Sarah Horne.
Description: First American edition. | New York : Henry Holt and
Company, 2016. | Series: Puppy Academy | Summary: "Everyone says
Star is much too fast to be a sheepdog, but when your mom is a sheepdog
champion, what else can you be? When a lamb goes missing on a field trip
to Stormy Mountain, Star races up to find it. But she soon discovers that the
lamb isn't the only one who needs her help" —Provided by publisher.
Identifiers: LCCN 2015042695 (print) | LCCN 2016021395 (ebook) |
ISBN 9781627797962 (hardback) | ISBN 9781627798037 (trade
paperback) | ISBN 9781627797979 (Ebook)
Subjects: | CYAC: Dogs—Fiction. | Animals—Infancy—Fiction. |
Sheep—Fiction. | Rescues—Fiction. | Working dogs—Fiction. | BISAC:
JUVENILE FICTION / Animals / Dogs. | JUVENILE FICTION / Action &
Adventure / General. | JUVENILE FICTION / Humorous Stories.
Classification: LCC PZ7.L58537 St 2016 (print) | LCC PZ7.L58537
(ebook) | DDC [Fic]—dc23
LC record available at https://lccn.loc.gov/2015042695

Our books may be purchased in bulk for promotional, educational,
or business use. Please contact your local bookseller or the Macmillan
Corporate and Premium Sales Department at (800) 221-7945 ext. 5442
or by e-mail at MacmillanSpecialMarkets@macmillan.com.

Originally published in the UK in 2015 by Oxford University Press
First American edition—2016

Printed in the United States of America by
R. R. Donnelley & Sons Company, Harrisonburg, Virginia

1 3 5 7 9 10 8 6 4 2 (hardcover)
1 3 5 7 9 10 8 6 4 2 (paperback)

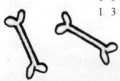

SCOUT
the smart one!

BREED: German Shepherd

SPECIAL SKILL:
Sniffing out
crime

PIP
the friendly one!

BREED: Labrador
retriever

SPECIAL SKILL:
Ball games

MURPHY
the big one!

BREED: Leonberger

SPECIAL SKILL:
Swimming

MAJOR BONES

One of the teachers at the
Sausage Dreams Puppy
Academy. Known for
being strict.

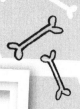

PROFESSOR OFFENBACH

Head of the Sausage
Dreams Puppy Academy.
She is a small dog with
A VERY LOUD VOICE!

1

The collie pups—Star, Gwen, Nevis, and Shep—pushed their way to the front of the crowd gathered at the bottom of the hill. A hushed silence fell across the dogs and humans who were watching. It was the final round of the National Sheepdog Trials, and it looked like Bleak Tarn, the old, gnarled collie and five-time champion, would win again.

But there was one dog remaining—
one dog who still had to run the
course.

Gwen nudged Star with her paw.
"Look—here comes your mom."

The pups watched Star's mom,
Lillabelle of Langdale Pike, trot
alongside her shepherd. The black-
and-white collie waited at the starting
line for the signal, and then she

was off. She raced up the hillside in a long curve toward the small flock of sheep grazing in the far field. She leaped the low wall and came up behind the sheep, slowing down as she did so. She knew that if she ran in too fast, she would scare them and they would scatter. The sheep saw her and drew together. Lillabelle kept her head low and crept closer to them, and the small flock set off steadily down the hillside toward the crowd.

"That was perfect!" said Nevis.

"If the rest of the trial goes this well, your mom might win," said Shep.

Lillabelle guided the sheep through
narrow gates, then drove them into
a circle marked on the ground.
Next, she had to single out the ewe
with the green spot painted on her
back. She circled the sheep, keeping
them in a tight group, and when
she saw the ewe on the outside of
the flock, she swiftly trotted in and
herded it away.

The crowd held their breath.

Maybe Lillabelle's performance was good enough to beat Bleak Tarn, but there was one last part of the trial to complete. It was the most difficult part of all. Lillabelle had to herd the sheep into the square pen and shut the gate. It wouldn't be easy. The sheep were getting bored and restless. They wanted to be back out on the hillside with the other flocks.

Lillabelle kept them calm. If she charged in now, all would be lost. She tried to forget the crowd watching her. She also tried to forget Bleak Tarn, who would be willing her to fail.

Keeping her belly low to the
ground, she crept forward. The
sheep bunched together more
tightly, looking for an escape route
to the hillside. But Lillabelle kept
them moving, and before they knew
it, the sheep had followed one
another into the pen. The shepherd

swung the gate shut, and the crowd exploded with applause.

She had done it. Bleak Tarn had been beaten at last.

There was a new winner now.

A new champion.

Lillabelle of Langdale Pike had won the National Sheepdog Trials.

 7

Gwen turned to Star. "Your mom is awesome," she said.

"The best!" said Shep.

"My dad said she would win," said Nevis.

Star puffed out her chest in pride. Her mom was a champion sheepdog. Everyone said Star would be a champion too. Star hoped so. She hoped one day she would win the National Sheepdog Trials and make her mom proud.

Star was looking forward to
tomorrow. Tomorrow was the
beginning of the pups' sheepdog
training, and Star couldn't
wait.

The next morning, Star, Gwen,
Nevis, and Shep gathered in the
classroom.

"Right," said Major Bones. "It's
time to get started on your basic
sheepherding skills. We'll go out to
the field and see if Hilda and Mabel
are ready for us."

The four collie pups followed
Major Bones outside. Major Bones

was a teacher at the Sausage Dreams
Puppy Academy for Working Dogs.
There were all sorts of puppies at the
Puppy Academy. There were pups who
were training to be guide dogs, pups
who wanted to be hearing dogs (to
help people who are deaf), and pups
who wanted to be water-rescue dogs.
But Star wanted to be a sheepdog

like her mom. She was a border collie, after all, and border collies had sheepherding in their blood.

Hilda and Mabel, the academy sheep, weren't in the field. They were in the barn, sitting on hay bales, chitchatting and knitting woolen blankets for dogs in rescue shelters.

"Ooh, hello, my dears," Hilda bleated, seeing the collie pups.

"Hello," baa-ed Mabel.

Hilda put her knitting down. "Well, if it isn't little Gwen, Shep, Nevis, and Star," she bleated. She gave Star a little wink. "We're expecting great things from you."

"Great things," baa-ed Mabel in agreement.

Star smiled to herself. She imagined winning the National Sheepdog Trials: Star of Langdale Pike, the new champion.

"No need for idle talk," barked Major Bones. "Let's get started."

"Right-ho, right-ho," bleated Hilda. "Just give me time. My legs don't move as fast as they used to."

"Not as fast," baa-ed Mabel.

They climbed down from their hay bales and hobbled outside into the field.

Hilda and Mabel had lived at the Puppy Academy longer than anyone could remember and had taught many young collies the basics of herding sheep. They were gentle, kind, and patient sheep, although they could manage only a slow shuffle around the field these days.

"Now then, young'uns," said

Hilda, "Mabel and I will stand over there." She pointed to the far end of the field. "And you have to run around us and drive us through that gate and into that pen there."

"That pen there," baa-ed Mabel.

"Remember," said Hilda, "run a wide curve and keep it nice and steady."

"Nice and steady," baa-ed Mabel.

Star watched Hilda and Mabel totter across the field. She could feel excitement fizz through her. She was about to herd sheep for the first time—ever. Her paws twitched. Her nose twitched. Her muscles

felt like coiled springs just waiting to
bounce.

Star was the last to take her turn.
She watched Gwen, then Nevis, then
Shep, herd Hilda and Mabel across the
field and into the pen. Once or twice,
Hilda pretended to hobble away but
let the pups herd her back again.

All the time Star was watching them, she felt her muscles tighten even more. She wanted it to be her turn. She wanted to be herding Hilda and Mabel. Her heart thumped inside her chest. The tip of her tail tingled with excitement. She couldn't keep her feet still. She jumped up and down on the spot.

Major Bones waited for Hilda and Mabel to shuffle back to the far end of the field, and then he turned to Star. But before he could say GO, Star was off, streaking across the field in a blur of black-and-white fur. She leaped the fence, did a midair half spin, and flew like a bullet toward Hilda and Mabel.

"Ooh, heavens!" bleated Hilda, breaking into a trot.

"Oh, lordy!" baa-ed Mabel, running off in a different direction.

Star ran around them to herd them up again.

Lordy!

"Ooh, me knees," bleated Hilda, stumbling on a rock.

"Slow down, young'un," baa-ed Mabel. "We're not spring lambs anymore."

But Star couldn't slow down. She was a sheepdog, and she had to herd these sheep. She ran around them in circles to keep them together. Round and round. Faster and faster. Round and round and round and round and round and round and round and round and round and round.

"Ooh! I'm quite dizzy," bleated Hilda.

"My head's spinning," baa-ed Mabel. "I think I need to lie down."

"Me too, dear," agreed Hilda.

"STAR!" bellowed Major Bones. "Come back at once."

Star stopped running. She looked back at Major Bones and then at Hilda and Mabel. What had she done? She hadn't even managed to herd them through the gates. She watched the two old ewes head back to the barn in dizzy circles.

Gwen, Shep, and Nevis were staring at her with their mouths wide open.

Star was supposed to be a sheepdog, the daughter of a champion, but her first attempt at herding had gone horribly, horribly wrong.

2

"Too fast," bleated Hilda.

"Much too faaaast," baa-ed Mabel. "You almost frightened the wool off my back."

Star sat down next to the two sheep, who were lying in deep straw—recovering.

"I didn't mean to scare you," said Star.

"We know that, my dear," said Hilda, "but other sheep won't. If you

go in so fast, they will think you're
about to attack them. You're not a
wolf, my dear. You are a border collie
with sheepherding in your blood.
You've got to go in slowly and calmly."

"Calmly," repeated Mabel. "I
remember your mom when she was a
young pup. Soft and gentle she was.
Paws like velvet."

Star stared at her own
paws. They twitched

with energy. They wanted to be running, running, running. They wanted to jump and spring and bounce. How could she ever be like her mom? She had so much to live up to.

"Don't worry," said Gwen at playtime. "It will be better next time, I'm sure."

"But we won't be herding sheep," said Nevis.

Star frowned. "Why not?"

"The vet said Hilda and Mabel need a long rest after today."

Shep pricked up his ears. "What will we be herding?"

Nevis looked at them all. "Haven't you heard? We'll be trying for our Level One Bo-Peep badge at the end of the week. But instead of sheep, we'll be herding . . . ducks!"

"Ducks?" said Star.

"Ducks?" said Shep.

"Those quacky things?" said Gwen.

"Yes, ducks," said Major Bones. "Not exactly ideal, but they're the best we can do under the circumstances. I had a word with a few of the village ducks on the pond, and they said they'd do it for a bag of grain."

"But we're sheepdogs," said Star, "not duck-dogs!"

"A true border collie can herd anything," said Major Bones gruffly. "Why, I remember the time your mother herded some human toddlers away from a busy road and back into a park."

Star sighed. She looked enviously at Gwen, Nevis, and Shep. They

were never compared with anyone. Sometimes she wished her mom weren't the National Sheepdog Champion.

Star worried all week. The Level One Bo-Peep badge was easy. Everyone said so. In fact, no one had failed it. But Star chased her tail in worry. She wished Hilda and Mabel would be there to help instead of the ducks. She'd never found the village ducks particularly friendly. They spent most of their time in the water with their bottoms in the air, ignoring everyone.

It was the end of the week. Friends and family had arrived to watch the pups take their Level One Bo-Peep badge. Star had been practicing all week, running the course with imaginary sheep. She saw her mom and waved a paw. She wondered if the other parents expected Star to be as brilliant as her mom. She wished there weren't so many people watching.

"Quack!" said the ducks crossly. "Quack . . . quack . . . quack . . . quack, quack . . . "

The ducks gathered in an angry group in the middle of the field. Clearly they didn't want to be there. They had only come for the food.

"Quack . . . quack, quack . . ."

"WELCOME," yapped Professor Offenbach.

Professor Offenbach was the head of the school. She was a small dog with a loud voice. Too loud, most people said, although no one dared tell Professor Offenbach that.

"WELCOME, FRIENDS AND FAMILY, ON THIS GLORIOUS AFTERNOON. TODAY IS A VERY SPECIAL DAY. OUR FOUR YOUNG PUPS WILL BE SHOWING THEIR DUCK—ER, SHEEPDOG SKILLS. IN THE CROWD, WE HAVE NONE OTHER THAN THE NATIONAL CHAMPION, LILLABELLE OF LANGDALE PIKE."

A ripple of applause spread across the crowd.

Professor Offenbach glanced directly at Star. **"LET'S HOPE SOME OF THAT TALENT HAS RUBBED OFF ON**

A FEW OF OUR YOUNG PUPS
TODAY."

Star watched Gwen, Nevis, and
Shep take their turns. The ducks
were an awkward bunch, running
this way and that, quacking rudely
at everyone. But each of the pups

managed to coax them across the
field, through the gates, and into
the holding pen, where Major
Bones had scattered some grain to
encourage them to go in.

Star waited for her turn. Her whole body trembled. Her paws twitched. Her nose twitched. Her eyes focused on the rowdy ducks. They were dabbling in a puddle in the middle of the field, squabbling over the muddiest bit. *Go in slow on velvet feet*, Star told herself. But her body wasn't listening. Her feet wanted to run and run and run.

She was off, racing like a greyhound toward the ducks, her feet flying across the grass, her paws barely touching the ground. She leaped the gate with plenty of room to spare. Too high! Too fast! She went skidding and skittering out of control. Round and round and round she spun.

BAM!

Feathers and mud flew into the air, and Star landed with her face in the puddle.

She picked herself up. It hadn't been the greatest of starts, but she hadn't finished yet. Maybe she could still herd the ducks into the pen. Maybe she could still save face and earn her Level One Bo-Peep badge.

When the mud and feathers settled, Star looked around for the ducks. But they were nowhere to be seen. Nowhere at all. It was as if

they had vanished into thin air.

Star looked up. High in the sky, the ducks were getting smaller and smaller and smaller as they flapped away toward the village.

Star felt everyone watching her. She had nothing to herd now. She wouldn't get her Level One Bo-Peep badge. She would be the first puppy in the academy to fail it. She couldn't face any of the other pups. She couldn't face her mom, either. Star scrambled up

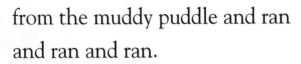

from the muddy puddle and ran
and ran and ran.

"Funny things, ducks," bleated
Hilda.

"Temperamental," agreed
Mabel.

"They flew away," wailed Star.

"It's their wings that does it,"
bleated Hilda.

"Wings!" baa-ed Mabel.

Star flumped down in the
straw. "What was I meant to
do? Sprout wings too?"

"Star?"

Star looked up. Her mother

had found her hiding in the barn with the sheep.

Star put her head in her paws. "You're mad at me, aren't you? I've failed. I didn't pass the test."

Lillabelle sat down next to her. "Of course I'm not mad. It was only one test. It doesn't matter."

"But I can't herd," cried Star. "I'm too fast."

"Too fast," bleated Hilda.

"Like a rocket," baa-ed Mabel. "An out-of-control rocket," she added as an afterthought.

"It's just excitement," said Lillabelle. "You'll learn."

Star curled herself into a ball. "But you never rushed in when you were young. I'll never be like you."

"Star," said Lillabelle softly, "I don't want you to be like me. I want you to be you."

"You mean fast and bouncy and unable to keep still?" said Star crossly. "Who wants a sheepdog like that?"

"You don't even have to be a sheepdog." Lillabelle sighed. "Just because I am doesn't mean you have to be."

"But what else can I be? I don't want to be a pampered pooch in the city. I want to be outside, running in the hills."

Lillabelle put a paw on Star's shoulder. "Star, you have many, many talents. One day, you will find out what they're for."

But Star wasn't listening. She had

covered her ears with her paws. She
was useless. She couldn't even herd
two old sheep or a few rowdy ducks.
What hope did she have of herding a
huge flock of five hundred or more
sheep? She was no good at anything
at all.

3

"All aboard," woofed Major Bones.

Star climbed into the van with the other collie pups.

Today they were heading off to Hilltop Farm, in the mountains, to earn their Mountain Shepherd badge. They would be herding sheep down from the high hills.

Star sat next to Gwen and looked nervously out the window. "How many sheep do you think we will have to herd today?" she asked.

"They have huge flocks in the mountains," said Gwen.

"Oh," said Star. "I can't even herd a few ducks."

"Don't worry," said Gwen. "You just had a bad day. Anyway, I heard Mabel say we don't have to herd the mountain sheep by ourselves. We'll do it as a team."

"At least they won't have wings," said Shep.

"We'll help each other," said Nevis.

But Star was worried. The others seemed much better than she was at herding. Would it really be that easy, working as a team?

The journey took a long, long time. Star hated having to sit still. Her legs twitched with energy. After midday, the van began to climb up toward the mountains. The road became steeper and steeper and narrower and narrower. Green fields gave way to wide-open mountain slopes of coarse, stubby grass and trickling streams.

"Sheep," said Gwen.

"Sheep," said Nevis.

"Sheep," said Shep.

They couldn't take their eyes off all the sheep. So many sheep. They had never seen so many together at one time.

But Star wasn't looking at the sheep. She was looking up at the mountains, at the way the clouds swirled and danced across the snowcapped peaks. She was looking at the high ridges and the tumbling waterfalls.

She was looking at the way the sunlight played on the dark, wet rock. What would it be like to run up the mountains and feel the sun and the wind in her fur? She wanted to be up there—up in the clouds, higher than the birds. She wanted to stand on the very top of the world.

"Star," said Gwen, giving her a poke.

Star pulled herself away from the mountains.

"Look, there's Hilltop Farm," said Gwen.

In the distance, a farmhouse sat at the base of the highest mountain. Major Bones turned off the main road and into the farm's driveway. They bounced and bumped, climbing higher and higher, while the countryside around them became wilder and wilder.

"Oh no," said Nevis, shrinking back from the window.

"What?" said Shep.

"If I'm not mistaken, those are Herdwick sheep."

"So?" said Gwen.

Nevis started to tremble. "My dad told me that Herdwick are the toughest, meanest, scariest sheep of all."

Outside, the Herdwick sheep glared at them as they passed.

All the pups sank lower in their seats. They wished Hilda and Mabel were there instead.

"Welcome to Hilltop Farm." An old, shaggy collie was waiting for them. Thick clumps of hardened mud stuck to the ends of his long fur and clunked together like chimes in the swirling wind. He had a graying muzzle and an eye patch over his right eye. His left eye was as pale as the winter sky.

"Good day, Angus," said Major
Bones, shaking his paw.

"Is it?" said Angus, casting his one
eye up at the sky. "There's snow in the
air. I can feel it."

Gwen looked up at the blue sky.
There was hardly a cloud in sight. It
didn't look like it was going to snow
today.

"I know what you're thinking,
wee lassie," said Angus. "But you're
in the mountains now." He paused,
looking slowly at each of them. "And
mountains have their own ideas about
the weather."

The puppies huddled closer
together.

 49

Angus lowered his voice, as if he didn't want the hills to hear. He pointed to the craggy peak looming above them. "And that there is Stormy Mountain."

"Stormy Mountain?" whispered Star.

"Aye," said Angus. "It lives up to its name. You wouldn't want to be up there when the clouds come down."

Star felt a thin chill of wind curl around her and ruffle her fur. She looked up at the mountain towering above the farmhouse. Wisps of snow whipped up from the mountaintop and swirled in the air. Deep down, Star knew Angus was right. She felt

it in her bones. She wasn't sure how, but she just knew a snowstorm was coming.

"Well, let's get ye all to the barn for a hot drink before we start," said Angus.

Star, Nevis, Shep, and Gwen followed Major Bones and Angus across the farmyard and toward the barn.

"What's with the eye patch?" whispered Shep to Nevis.

Angus stopped. He turned around

4

In the short time it took to reach
the barn, the first few flurries of
snow began to fall.

"Now then," said Angus. He
pointed to a map of the farm. "For
your Mountain Shepherd badge, you
have to gather the sheep and their
lambs up here and herd them down
the hill, across the stream, along the
path, and into the farmyard here.
We'll be working as a team, but I
will be judging you individually."

Gwen, Shep, and Nevis looked at the route Angus had shown them. But Star was looking at the footpaths and sheep tracks that crisscrossed the mountain. Some of the paths led to the very top.

"What about the rams?" said Shep.

"There'll be no rams in the flock today," said Angus. "But you'll have to keep an eye out for ramblers."

"Ramblers?" said Star. She'd never heard of ramblers. "Are they dangerous too?"

"No, wee lassie," said Angus. "Ramblers just get in the way sometimes, that's all. They're people who like to walk up the mountains."

He pointed through the barn doors
to where a group of people in bright
waterproof jackets and pants and
big leather boots tromped across the
yard. They were carrying knapsacks
and maps, and the one in front was
holding a compass.

"What do they do when they get
to the top?" asked Nevis.

"Well," said Angus, "they have a look around for a bit and then come back down again."

Gwen frowned. "What's the point in that?"

"Humans are crazy," said Nevis. "That's what my dad says."

Star watched the people head up into the hills. She didn't think they were crazy. She wanted to climb up the mountain too. She wanted to race across the high ridges and see the whole world laid out before her.

A thin layer of snow coated the ground as they made their way up the steep mountain path. The sheep and lambs were scattered across the hillside. Star tried to count them all. She reached two hundred but then lost count. *Too many to count,* she thought. *How could Angus keep watch over them all?*

In a lower field, a ram with a scarred face and a tattooed ear glared at them as they passed. Nevis stopped to look. He couldn't help staring at the ram's huge, curly horns.

"Oi, fluff ball! What are you looking at?" the ram baa-ed angrily.

Nevis hurried to catch up with the other pups, his tail between his legs. He hoped the ewes wouldn't be quite so scary. At least they didn't have horns.

Star watched the ramblers heading up Stormy Mountain. Some were in small groups. There were others walking alone. She counted ten people in all. People were easier to count than sheep. She secretly wished she could join them.

Angus led the pups across the hills to the lower slopes of the mountain. "We'll need to bring all the sheep down today. There's bad weather on the way, and the lambs might not survive the night if they're caught out here."

Star looked up. Thick white clouds now lay across the sky like a heavy blanket. Flakes of snow swirled down like feathers, covering the ground. Only the long, spiky blades of grass showed through.

Angus sent the pups in different directions to gather the sheep and bring them all together in one big flock. Star was sent to the high slopes, to a stone wall separating the farm from the rest of the mountain.

Star had been waiting for this moment all day. She had been cooped up in the van for too long, and now her legs wanted to run and run. The sheep at the top were happily munching on lichens and moss. They didn't see Star coming. But suddenly they heard her feet racing across the ground, leaping from rock to rock, flying like a rocket toward them.

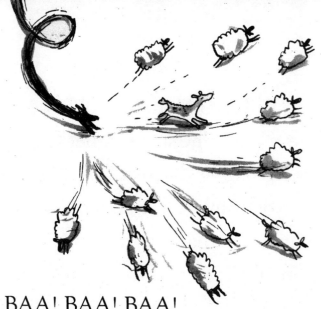

BAA! BAA! BAA!
BAA! BAA! BAA!

The lambs panicked. They scattered
in all directions, their mothers
galloping after them.

Oh no! thought Star. *I'm losing them.*
She ran faster, circling round and
round them, but the lambs panicked
even more, scrambled over the wall,
and charged off up the hillside.

"YOUNG PUP!" An old ewe barred Star's way. She stamped her foot and snorted. She glared at Star. "Just what do you think you're doing, scaring the lambs like that? Do you want them to run off the edge of the mountain?"

Star sat down. She stared at her feet. Why did she have to be so fast? Why couldn't she control herself?

Other sheep started to crowd around Star in a circle. "It's no way for a

border collie to behave," baa-ed one.

"A disgrace," baa-ed another, "leaping around like a wild thing."

One ewe narrowed her eyes at Star. "There's always a bad one—a wolf in every pack."

Star trembled as the angry flock of sheep closed in around her.

"Ahem!" Angus pushed his way through. "Now, ladies," he said. "Break it up. Break it up. There's snow coming. Let's gather up the lambs and head down to the farm."

The old ewe stamped her foot at Angus.

"Please," he added.

"That's better," she said. "Right, girls, gather up your lambs. The old dog's right. Snow's a-coming, and we'd better tuck our young'uns in the barn for the night." She put her head in the air, ignoring Star, and trotted down the hillside with her lamb. The other sheep and lambs followed, glaring at Star with disgust.

Star looked up at Angus. She could see sympathy in his old face.

"Too fast. I know," said Star. She turned and walked away, her head down and her tail between her legs.

The snow was falling faster now, building against the stone walls in thick drifts.

Angus caught up with her. "I hope you don't mind," he said, "but I think it's better if you let the other pups bring the sheep down. It'll be dark soon enough, and we don't want to lose any lambs on the mountain tonight."

Star nodded miserably. There was no way she could earn her Mountain Shepherd badge now.

5

Star stayed at the back of the flock
and watched as the other pups built
up their confidence, running this
way and that, keeping the sheep
together. She followed at a distance
as they came down from the hills,
crossed the stream, and joined
the ramblers returning from the
mountain. The weather was closing
in. No one, it seemed, wanted to be
stuck on the mountain tonight.

The sheep and lambs trotted into the warm light of the barn and began to munch on the sweet hay. Angus stood on a haystack and surveyed them all. "Good job," he said to Gwen, Nevis, and Shep. He looked out at the swirling snow in the darkening sky. "We got them back home in time."

Star knew they'd have to go back home to the academy soon too, dashing her dreams of getting a Mountain Shepherd badge. Maybe she would never be a sheepdog. She was walking toward the barn doors when an old ewe shoved past, bowling her over.

"BAA!" cried the ewe. "Laaaamb!"

"Lamb?" said Star.

The old ewe looked frantically at the other sheep. "I can't find my lamb. Laaamb!" she bleated across the barn. She ran back to the doors. "LAAAAAAMB!" she bleated into the snowstorm. The wind whipped her bleat away, but there was no returning reply.

Angus looked worried. "We must've lost one on the way down," he said.

"Laaamb," wailed the ewe.

Before anyone could stop her, Star was gone, racing out into the gathering darkness, racing out into the storm. Her feet flew across the snow as she retraced their path. She leaped across the stream, circling and sniffing to find the lost lamb. Just beyond the stream, a set of tiny hoofprints left the path. They headed up, up, up, back toward the mountain. The hoofprints went round and round in circles. Star knew this lamb was lost and trying to find its way home.

"Woof," she barked. "Woof!"

A muffled "baa" replied.

Star ran, pounding through the thick snow. If she didn't find the lamb soon, the new snow would cover the prints and they would be lost forever.

At last, she found the lamb lying in a snowdrift, buried in snow, unable to climb out. The lamb was cold and wet through.

"Come on," woofed Star. She put her nose underneath the lamb and pushed it out of the snowdrift.

The lamb struggled to its feet and wobbled after Star. Star waited for it, and together they made their way down the path.

The wind whirled around them. The lamb was weak, but Star gently nudged it down the hill. Sometimes the blizzard blew so fiercely that Star couldn't see her way at all, but she'd kept the map of the mountain in her head, and so she found her way back down.

"Star, is that you?"

"BAAAA!"

Angus, Major Bones, and the old ewe were on their way up the path to meet them. The ewe rushed to her lamb.

"Well done," said Angus. "Your swift feet saved this young lamb."

"Well done, indeed," said Major Bones.

Star sighed. She was glad she'd saved the lamb, but she'd never be a true sheepdog if she couldn't control her feet.

Star followed them down the mountainside and along the main path to the farmyard. The snow had stopped, and a thin sliver of moon peeped through the clouds, lighting the mountaintops. Star stopped to look. She had never seen anything so beautiful. The snow seemed to glow against the dark, star-scattered sky. She wanted to be up there, racing beneath the moonlight across the powdery snow.

"Come on, Star, keep up," woofed Major Bones.

Star turned and trotted down the path. Ramblers' footprints and sheep hoofprints all mixed together in the snow. The rubber soles of the ramblers' boots all left different prints. Star counted nine sets of prints coming down the mountain.

Nine?

She checked again.

She felt a knot of worry tighten in her chest. Her paws twitched.

There were only nine sets coming down, but Star remembered that ten people had gone up the mountain.

She looked back up at the towering peak.

Someone hadn't returned.

Someone was still up there, on the mountain.

It was dark and cold, and another snowstorm was coming.

"Star!" Major Bones called again.

"Someone's stuck on Stormy Mountain," Star called out.

"Star, come back!"

But it was too late. Star was already racing up, up, up the mountain path. Before Major Bones could call her name again, Star had disappeared into the velvet darkness of the night.

6

The path seemed to go on forever.
Star followed the cairns—the piles
of rocks left by walkers to mark the
path. It was much colder up on
the mountain, and the wind blew
through her coat like sharp needles
of ice. Up, up, up she scrambled until
she could go no farther. The whole
of the world was spread out before
her.

The warm orange glow of the barn

light lay far, far below in the moonlit valley.

This was what it was like to stand at the very top of the world. Star wanted to stay longer, but she knew there wasn't time.

Star sniffed around. She picked out lots of human scents and then found one that headed away from the main path, off on its own. She followed it as it went round and round in circles, like the lamb's

hoofprints had. This person was lost too.

Star followed the scent to a ridge that led down the other side of the mountain. But the trail continued to the steep edge of the ridge, as if someone had walked off the mountain and into thin air.

Star crept closer to the edge. She looked over into the darkness. On a thin ledge below her, she could see a lumpy shape. The shape groaned and moved.

It was a young man.

The lost rambler!

He must have fallen over the edge.

"Woof," barked Star.

The rambler turned to look at her.
Star could see he was hurt. His leg
stuck out at a very odd angle. She
scrambled down the rocks, leaping
lightly across them.

"Woof," she barked again. "Woof."

The man took hold of her. "Good
dog," he said. "Good dog."

Star could feel his hands trembling. They were cold, so cold.

Star knew she wouldn't be able to help the man up. Even if he could walk, he wouldn't be able to climb back onto the ridge above. It was too high and too steep for him.

Star didn't know what to do. She wanted to tell him to wait and she'd find help, but she knew humans didn't understand her woofs and barks.

She couldn't leave the man alone. She sat beside him, trying to keep him warm, but his eyes kept closing. She knew that if he fell asleep, he might roll right off the narrow ledge. She pawed at him and whined, trying to keep him awake. But the night was getting colder. Even with her thick coat, Star could feel the wind's icy fingers. Ice crystals formed on her whiskers, and her breath froze and sparkled in the night air. Somehow she had to get the rambler off the mountain, but how? She knew for sure that he wouldn't survive up here.

She stared out across the valley. What could she do? Her wolf ancestors would have howled across the mountains to find one another. Maybe that was what

she needed to try. Star threw
back her head and howled. She
howled like the ancient wolf that
was somewhere deep inside her.
"AAAAArrrrrOOOOOOOOOO!
AAArrrrrOOOOOOOOOO!"

From far, far below came the baying
of dogs in reply.

It was Angus and Major Bones.
They were coming up the mountain
to find her.

AAROOOo

Major Bones and Angus were soon panting on the ridge above Star and the rambler.

Star bounded up the rocks to meet them, her paws light on the crumbly rocks.

"I think his leg is broken," woofed Star.

Major Bones tried to climb down. He put a paw on one of the rocks, but the rock slipped under his weight and went tumbling and bouncing down into the darkness.

"We can't reach him," woofed Major Bones.

"Too far down," said Angus.

"We can't leave him," said Star.

Major Bones pulled himself up to his full height. "Right. Let's go back to the farmhouse and get some help. We can't do this on our own."

Angus nodded. "I'll call Snowdon. He'll know what to do."

"Snowdon?" said Star.

"Yes," said Angus. "Come on! We don't have much time."

Star jumped back down onto the ledge. "I'll stay with the rambler," she said.

Major Bones looked at her. "We can't leave you here too," he said.

"Someone has to stay with him,"

said Star. "Someone needs to keep him warm and awake, and I'm the only one who can get down here."

Major Bones didn't look happy, but he agreed. "Right," he said. "We'll be as fast as we can."

Star huddled next to the rambler to keep him warm.
It was even colder

now, and it had begun to snow again. The clouds covered the moon, plunging Star and the young man into deep, deep darkness. Every time the rambler drifted off to sleep, Star woofed to wake him.

Star wondered when help would come. She knew Major Bones and Angus wouldn't forget her, but it seemed so long since they had left to get help. She was cold, and tired too— so tired. She knew she mustn't sleep, but maybe she could have a little nap. *Just a short one*, she told herself. She was drifting into sleep when she saw a light high up in the sky.

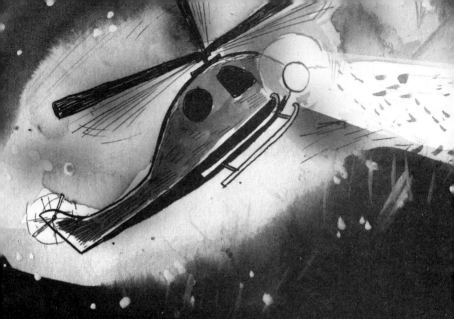

Ducks? she thought drowsily.
Ducks with headlights?

If they were ducks, they were
very noisy ducks, as if hundreds
of wings beat together at
once.

Star opened her eyes wide.
"Helicopter," she woofed. "Helicopter,
helicopter, helicopter."

The rambler rubbed his eyes.

"Helicopter," Star barked again.

The helicopter's light was sweeping across the mountainside, looking for them.

"Over here," Star barked. But she knew the pilot wouldn't be able to hear her above the noise of the helicopter blades. She watched as

the helicopter swung away
and started to search another
part of the mountain. The
clouds were coming down again,
and the wind was getting stronger.
The helicopter couldn't fly in thick
clouds. If it didn't find Star and the
rambler soon, it would have to leave
them on Stormy Mountain and
come back the next morning.

But the next morning might be
too late.

The rambler stirred. He fumbled
for something in his pocket. He
pulled out a small flashlight and
switched it on, but his hands were
so cold, he couldn't hold

on to it. The flashlight slipped from his fingers. Star watched it tumble and bounce onto a narrower ledge below, its light hidden by a rock. She knew that if she climbed down, she might not be able to get back up. But this might be their only chance.

Skittering down the slope, she reached the flashlight and held it up. She pointed its beam into the darkness, where it shone as bright as any star.

The helicopter turned back, and its light found Star and the rambler clinging to the mountain.

Star pressed herself against the rocks as the wind from the helicopter blades blew against her. She watched a man drop down on a long wire and strap the rambler onto a stretcher.

"Come on, girl," the rescuer said, holding out his arms to Star. "We'll take you back with us too."

Star clung to the man as the winch lifted them higher and higher, right into the helicopter.

"Well done, young'un," said a voice behind her.

Star turned. A big border collie wrapped a blanket around her. She couldn't help staring at him. What was a dog doing in the helicopter? The collie was wearing a bright red reflective jacket. Star had never seen such a thing before.

"Who are you?" asked Star. "What are you doing here?"

"I'm Snowdon," said the collie. "I'm with the Mountain Search and Rescue Team."

7

All the puppies at the academy gathered for the Friday award ceremony. Friends and family were there to watch too. Star sat at the very back. She could see her mom looking for her, but she hid down behind Wolfie, the wolfhound pup. She didn't want to face her mom knowing she hadn't earned her Mountain Shepherd badge.

Professor Offenbach climbed onto the stage.

"WE HAVE QUITE A FEW AWARDS AND BADGES TO GET THROUGH TODAY," she barked.

"FIRST, I'D LIKE TO CALL UP WOLFIE FOR HIS ACTING PERFORMANCE AS THE WOLF IN THE VILLAGE PLAY OF 'LITTLE RED RIDING HOOD.' EVERYONE SAID HE PLAYED THE ROLE EXTREMELY WELL." Professor Offenbach coughed. "TOO WELL, A FEW VILLAGERS SAID. WE ONLY HOPE THEY WILL FEEL SAFE ENOUGH TO LEAVE THEIR HOMES AFTER DARK AGAIN SOON."

Wolfie stood up to take his place on the giant sausage podium. Star glanced up to see her mom looking directly at her.

"AND NEXT," bellowed Professor Offenbach, "WE HAVE GWEN, NEVIS, AND SHEP, FOR ACHIEVING THEIR MOUNTAIN SHEPHERD BADGE."

Star watched her friends gather on the podium. She wished she could be up there with them. She couldn't even look at her mother. Star was the first border collie in a long line of border collies not good enough to be a sheepdog. She had failed.

Star half listened to other pups collecting their awards and badges. Maybe she could slip out of the ceremony. She didn't want to stay any longer.

"AND NOW . . . ," said Professor Offenbach, "WE HAVE A NEW AWARD. IT HAS NEVER BEEN PRESENTED TO ANY DOG AT THE ACADEMY BEFORE."

Star crept along the back of the
hall to sneak out.

"AND WE HAVE SOME SPECIAL
GUESTS TO AWARD IT."

There was a commotion up at the
front, and Star could see humans,
dogs, and sheep coming through
the doors. First was Angus, then the
old ewe with her lamb, followed by

the rambler in a wheelchair, the helicopter pilot, the rescuer, and Snowdon the mountain rescue dog.

"I WOULD LIKE TO CALL STAR, STAR OF LANGDALE PIKE, UP TO THE PODIUM," barked Professor Offenbach.

Star looked around. Did the professor really mean her?

"STAR, PLEASE COME TO THE PODIUM."

For the first time in her life, Star's feet didn't want to move. They felt like they were stuck in thick, thick molasses.

Gwen was waving her paw at her. "Come on, Star!"

"IN OUR FINE HISTORY AT THE ACADEMY, GUIDE DOGS, SHEEPDOGS, HEARING DOGS, AND MANY MORE HAVE PASSED THROUGH OUR GATES," woofed Professor Offenbach. "BUT TODAY, WE HAVE A NEW JOB TO RECOGNIZE."

All eyes were on Star as she
climbed up on the sausage podium.

"STAR HAS SHOWN MANY
EXCELLENT QUALITIES. SHE
HAS SPEED AND AGILITY. BUT
SHE HAS SOMETHING ELSE TOO:
BRAVERY AND TRUE LOYALTY
IN THE FACE OF DANGER. THE
MOUNTAIN RESCUE TEAM SAID

THEY HAD NEVER SEEN SUCH
BRAVERY BEFORE, AND THEY HAVE
AWARDED STAR THEIR HIGHEST
HONOR, THE MUNRO MEDAL."

Angus stepped forward to put the
medal around Star's neck.

Everyone cheered. Professor
Offenbach had to wave her paws to
quiet everyone down.

"AND," she continued, "THEY HAVE ASKED IF STAR WOULD CONSIDER TRAINING TO BE PART OF THEIR TEAM. THEY THINK SHE WILL BE THE PERFECT MOUNTAIN RESCUE DOG."

Star could hardly believe her ears. She could do

something where she could run and run and run across the mountains and feel the wild wind in her fur. Star was standing on the sausage podium, but she felt as if she were standing on the very top of the world.

Professor Offenbach turned to Star. **"WHAT DO YOU THINK, STAR? DO YOU WANT TO BE A MOUNTAIN RESCUE DOG ONE DAY?"**

"WOOF!" agreed Star. "WOOF! WOOF! WOOF!"

"AND JUST ONE THING MORE," said Professor Offenbach, beckoning the old Herdwick ewe onto the stage.

The old ewe climbed up and faced
Star. "The girls and I wanted to say
thank you for saving one of our little
lambs. We got together and made
you a present." She held up a woolen
coat. "Made of the finest Herdwick
wool," she bleated. "It's the warmest
wool in the whole world. It'll
keep you warm and dry out on any
mountain."

"Thank you," said Star, beaming. "Thank you."

Those Herdwick sheep weren't so scary after all.

When the ceremony was over, Star went to find some peace and quiet in the barn.

She lay down in the straw next to Hilda and Mabel.

"Ooh! It suits you," bleated Hilda, admiring the Herdwick coat.

"Suits you," baa-ed Mabel. "Lovely bit of cable knit, that."

"Star?"

Star looked up. Her mom had found her.

"I'm sorry," said Star.

Star's mom sat down next to her. "Sorry for what?"

Star stared at her paws. "I know we come from a long line of sheepdogs, but that's not what I want to be. I want to be a mountain rescue dog. I hope I can make you proud of me."

Lillabelle put her paw on Star. "I have never been more proud of you than I am today. What you did on the mountain was very, very brave. But it doesn't matter to me what you do or how well you do it. I just love you as you."

Star looked up at her mom.

"Really?"

"Really!" Lillabelle smiled and gave her a kiss. "Star, my little pup, you'll always be a champion to me."

PUPPY PLEDGE

I promise to be honest, brave, and true and serve my fellow dogs and humans too.

In peril, I will be your guide, walking with you by your side.

I am your eyes, your ears, your nose, through wind and rain and sun and snow. I'll be with you until the very end, your wet-nosed, waggy-tailed best, best friend.

Meet Fern, a real-life search and rescue dog!

Name
Fern

Age
9

Occupation
Search and rescue dog

Likes
Tennis ball games, Cheesy Bites snacks

Hates
Cats!

Fern uses her nose to search for missing people. She lets her handler know that she has found someone by barking.

Search and Rescue Dog Facts

Search and rescue dogs use their noses to find human scent, but their amazing sense of hearing and their ability to see in the dark can also help.

DID YOU KNOW?

It is thought that a single dog can accomplish the work of twenty to thirty human searchers.

Mountain rescue dogs like Star are air-scenting dogs. They pick up a scent on the air and follow it to its source.

DID YOU KNOW?

Rescue dogs who travel in helicopters, like Snowdon in the story, must have flight training!

Border collies like Star make great search and rescue dogs, but German shepherds, labradors, and spaniels are also popular.

DID YOU KNOW?

One of the earliest-known mountain rescue dogs was a Saint Bernard named Barry. He worked in Switzerland in the early 1800s and saved more than forty lives.

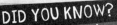

About Ned and his owner, Gill Lewis

I'm NED, a border collie just like Star. My mom was a champion sheepdog too. I was born on a farm in Devon along with seven brothers and sisters. Then I went to live with GILL LEWIS and her family. She doesn't have any sheep, but she does have chickens, and so I love rounding those up instead. I also love playing ball and Frisbee.

My feet never stop. I'm always running, running, running. I always need a job to do. If no one wants to play with me, I play with my best friend, Murphy, a Leonberger. He even puts up with me when I pull his tail. You will see him in a future Puppy Academy book.

But now you'll have to excuse me. I can't hang around here talking—I've got to run!

Don't miss

PUPPY ACADEMY

SCOUT
and the Sausage Thief

Gill Lewis

illustrations by Sarah Horne

More PUPPY ACADEMY
stories coming soon!

PIP
and the Paw of Friendship

MURPHY
and the Great Surf Rescue